12/04

1X(6/06) 3/09
1x (6/06) 3/12

CR

Ethnic Folklore

North American Folklore

Children's Folklore

Christmas and Santa Claus Folklore

Contemporary Folklore

Ethnic Folklore

Family Folklore

Firefighters' Folklore

Folk Arts and Crafts

Folk Customs

Folk Dance

Folk Fashion

Folk Festivals

Folk Games

Folk Medicine

Folk Music

Folk Proverbs and Riddles

Folk Religion

Folk Songs

Folk Speech

Folk Tales and Legends

Food Folklore

Regional Folklore

Ethnic Folklore

BY ELLYN SANNA

Mason Crest Publishers

Mason Crest Publishers Inc.
370 Reed Road
Broomall, Pennsylvania 19008
(866) MCP-BOOK (toll free)
www.masoncrest.com

First printing
1 2 3 4 5 6 7 8 9 10
Library of Congress Cataloging-in-Publication Data on file at the Library of Congress.
ISBN 1-59084-332-0
      1-59084-328-2 (series)

Design by Lori Holland.
Composition by Bytheway Publishing Services, Binghamton, New York.
Cover design by Joe Gilmore.
Printed and bound in the Hashemite Kingdom of Jordan.

Picture credits:
Artville: pp. 10, 12, 14, 18, 20
Comstock: p. 98
Eclectic Collection: p. 96
J. Rowe: pp. 16, 21, 26, 28, 36, 40, 44, 46, 56, 60, 88
Photo Alto: pp. 62, 64
PhotoDisc: pp. 6, 54, 70, 72, 75, 80, 82, 90, 94
Cover: "Gypsy Wagon" by Henry J. Soulen © 1936: SEPS: Licensed by Curtis Publishing, Indianapolis, IN. www.curtispublishing.com

Contents

Folklore grows from long-ago
seeds. Just as an acorn sends
down roots even as it shoots up
leaves across the sky, folklore is
rooted deeply in the past and
yet still lives and grows today.
It spreads through our modern
world with branches as wide
and sturdy as any oak's;
it grounds us in yesterday even
as it helps us make sense of
both the present and the future.

Introduction

by Dr. Alan Jabbour

WHAT DO A TALE, a joke, a fiddle tune, a quilt, a jig, a game of jacks, a saint's day procession, a snake fence, and a Halloween costume have in common? Not much, at first glance, but all these forms of human creativity are part of a zone of our cultural life and experience that we sometimes call "folklore."

The word "folklore" means the cultural traditions that are learned and passed along by ordinary people as part of the fabric of their lives and culture. Folklore may be passed along in verbal form, like the urban legend that we hear about from friends who assure us that it really happened to a friend of their cousin. Or it may be tunes or dance steps we pick up on the block, or ways of shaping things to use or admire out of materials readily available to us, like that quilt our aunt made. Often we acquire folklore without even fully realizing where or how we learned it.

Though we might imagine that the word "folklore" refers to cultural traditions from far away or long ago, we actually use and enjoy folklore as part of our own daily lives. It is often ordinary, yet we often remember and prize it because it seems somehow very special. Folklore is culture we share with others in our communities, and we build our identities through the sharing. Our first shared identity is family identity, and family folklore such as shared meals or prayers or songs helps us develop a sense of belonging. But as we grow older we learn to belong to other groups as well. Our identities may be ethnic, religious, occupational, or regional—or all of these, since no one has only one cultural identity. But in every case, the identity is anchored and strengthened by a variety of cultural traditions in which we participate and share with our neighbors. We feel the threads of connection with people we know, but the threads extend far beyond our own immediate communities. In a real sense, they connect us in one way or another to the world.

Folklore possesses features by which we distinguish ourselves from each other. A certain dance step may be African American, or a certain story urban, or a certain hymn Protestant, or a certain food preparation Cajun. Folklore can distinguish us, but at the same time it is one of the best ways we introduce ourselves to each other. We learn about new ethnic groups on the North American landscape by sampling their cuisine, and we enthusiastically adopt musical ideas from other communities. Stories, songs, and visual designs move from group to group, enriching all people in the process. Folklore thus is both a sign of identity, experienced as a special marker of our special groups, and at the same time a cultural coin that is well spent by sharing with others beyond our group boundaries.

Folklore is usually learned informally. Somebody, somewhere, taught us that jump rope rhyme we know, but we may have trouble remembering just where we got it, and it probably wasn't in a book that was assigned as homework. Our world has a domain of formal knowledge, but folklore is a domain of knowledge and culture that is learned by sharing and imitation rather than formal instruction. We can study it formally—that's what we are doing now!—but its natural arena is in the informal, person-to-person fabric of our lives.

Not all culture is folklore. Classical music, art sculpture, or great novels are forms of high art that may contain folklore but are not themselves folklore. Popular music or art may be built on folklore themes and traditions, but it addresses a much wider and more diverse audience than folk music or folk art. But even in the world of popular and mass culture, folklore keeps popping up around the margins. E-mail is not folklore—but an e-mail smile is. And college football is not folklore—but the wave we do at the stadium is.

This series of volumes explores the many faces of folklore throughout the North American continent. By illuminating the many aspects of folklore in our lives, we hope to help readers of the series to appreciate more fully the richness of the cultural fabric they either possess already or can easily encounter as they interact with their North American neighbors.

The arrival of the Spanish conquistadors in the New World brought two cultures together—and created a new folklore that was rooted in two separate, older ways of thinking.

ONE

Mirrors into Realty
The Folklore of North America's
Many Cultures

Immigrants to North America carried their folklore with them.

$\mathbf{A}$MERICA HAS often been called a melting pot—but that *metaphor* has a few problems. It implies that the various cultures brought by immigrants from other countries have all been absorbed into one *homogenous* substance. In reality, each ethnic group in North America has retained much of its original culture and traditions.

Ethnic folklore is not unchanged by its trip across the ocean, of course. Each group has influenced one another—and aspects of folklore and tradition have been modified to adapt to a new world, even as they have spread between groups. But the unique flavor of each ethnic group has never been lost.

The folklore from these groups is a little like a set of mirrors. The individual cultures use their folk traditions both to see themselves—and to reflect their identity to the larger world around them. As we look into this set of mirrors, we have a deeper understanding of North American culture as a whole.

The first immigrants to the North American continent were the many tribes we call Native Americans. These people had their own unique way of looking at the world, and their folklore reflects their perspectives. Centuries later, when Europeans began to cross the Atlantic, they brought with them a very different outlook, as well as entire bodies of folk stories and traditions that allow us to see into the worlds of the various European groups. Some of the Europeans brought with them people from Africa as slaves, and the African folk heritage further enriched the mix of cultures on the North American continent. Later waves of immigrants came from Asia, carrying with them yet another fresh per-

spective on reality and still another set of customs, beliefs, and stories.

As each group of immigrants reached North America, they found a world that was in many ways very different from the old worlds they had left behind. Their cultures encountered new demands, and they were influenced both by each other and by the land itself. No one coming from Europe had ever before encountered terrain that was as vast and untamed as the North American continent. At times, there seemed to be no room in this amazing, frightening, and bountiful new environment for their ancestors' myths and beliefs. Many may have wondered if their old gods, the ancient folklore and legends that had shaped their lives for generations, had been left behind on the other side of the ocean. Some traditions began to change or disappear, while new ones grew up in their place.

This process was reflected in the folklore "mirrors" of each culture—and of course as the image reflected by this set of mirrors changed, so did each group's sense of identity. For instance, when the Spanish arrived in the southwestern part of North America, they brought with them their Catholic faith with all its traditions and stories. As Spanish and native groups intermarried, a new ethnic identity was born—Hispanic American—and this group's

> Folklore is the boiled-down juice of human living.
>
> —*Zora Neale Hurston*

Native American folklore was influenced by the animals that inhabited their continent.

ARE THERE FAIRIES IN NORTH AMERICA?

One question that has always intrigued me is what happens to demonic beings when immigrants move from their homelands. Irish-Americans remember the fairies, Norwegian-Americans the *nisser*, Greek-Americans the *vrykólakas*, but only in relation to events remembered in the Old Country. When I once asked why such demons are not seen in America, my informants giggled confusedly and said, "They're scared to pass the ocean, it's too far". . . .

—Richard Dorson, *American Folklore and the Historian*

When Europeans brought the horse to North America, they changed the lives—and the folklore—of the native tribes.

folklore was a mixture of its two very different parents. One byproduct was Our Lady of Guadalupe, an Aztec goddess who blended with the Virgin Mary to create a brown-skinned, native Mary. Similar transformations occurred across the continent, as the various groups adapted to the New World while looking into each other's folk "mirrors."

North American folklore is full of mixtures like these, and yet all the while each ethnic group has held onto its own "mirror," its

No matter who you are, you have tradition of storytelling as your heritage. It may not be Native American; it may be Irish or Latvian, Japanese or Ashanti, but it is there. Look to the stories of your own birthright, and try to understand the lessons they teach you about your own life and the world around you.

—Joseph Bruchac, *Native American Stories*

If the distinct ingredients of the American experience have yet to blend in the real world pot (and would any of us enjoy a featureless gruel?), we can hope that in these pages the reader will find a nutritious and satisfying stew. . . .

—David Leeming and Jake Page, *Myths, Legends, and Folktales of America*

own way of reflecting the world and itself. The stories and traditions may have changed—but we can still catch a glimpse of the ancient original themes.

In our modern world, ethnic folklore is often forgotten. Our heads are filled with television programs and movie characters, and our society is a mobile one that has often lost its connection to family and community. But despite that, our ethnic heritage is still alive. For each ethnic  group, this legacy of folklore reveals and shapes reality's deepest meanings. It connects human beings to what is best and most significant about their lives. And it is a mirror that gives us a glimpse of both God and ourselves.

Native American folklore finds meaning
and life in the objects of nature.

TWO

Native American Folklore
Stories of Harmony and Balance

Kokopelli is a magical character who has fascinated humans since the first images of him were carved on stone walls 3,000 years ago. Today he is a popular image for jewelry and other designs.

LONG, LONG AGO, before the world we know today existed, there was another world, the First World. In that world, everything was dark, and only six beings lived in the darkness: First Man (who was the son of Night and the Blue Sky over the sunset), First Woman (who was the daughter of Day Break and the Yellow Sky of the sunrise), Salt Woman, Fire God, Coyote, and Begochiddy. Begochiddy was the Creator, the child of the Sun; he was both man and woman, and she had blue eyes and yellow hair.

Begochiddy began by making mountains in the darkness of First World. He made a white mountain in the east, a blue mountain in the south, a yellow mountain in the west, and a black mountain in the north. Then she made insects and plants to live on her mountains.

But things were out of balance in the First World. The Fire God was jealous of Begochiddy's creativity, and he began to destroy Begochiddy's creations with fire. The First Beings decided to leave First World and live somewhere else. They went to the red mountain, bringing the plants and insects with them, and there they climbed up one of Begochiddy's plants, up and up and up, until they reached the Second World.

Here Begochiddy created still more things—clouds, more plants, more mountains. The Second World was not dark like First World, but blue, and other beings lived there: Swallow People and Cat People. For a time everyone lived in harmony, but then, once again, things went out of kilter. People no longer got along, and the First People decided to climb up into yet another world.

The turtle is part of many native creation myths.

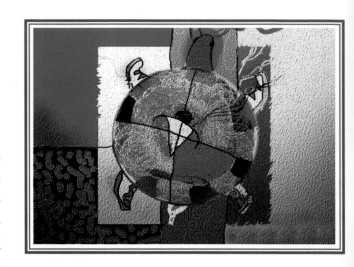

The Third World was yellow, because there the mountains gave off light. Begochiddy created rivers and water animals, birds and lightning. And then he made human beings, creatures who all spoke the same language. All creation understood one another and lived in harmony.

But although Third World was the most beautiful of any the worlds the First People had seen, it was not perfect, and it too lost its harmony. Evil diseases entered the world, and men and women began to argue with each other. Begochiddy knew she would have to lead creation up into yet another world.

The Third World was destroyed by a great flood, and Begochiddy gathered up all of creation and climbed the great plant that led up into the sky. This time, though, the journey was not as easy as before, for the plant stopped growing before it entered the Fourth World. Spider People wove a web, trying to bring the people closer to the next world, but they still could not break through the wall that separated them. Ant People tried to dig through the wall, but they were too small. Finally, the Locust used his hard head and broke into the Fourth World.

Begochiddy poked her head through and looked around. She found herself on an island,

Storytelling is an essential part of native folklore—but so is dance. Native Americans use dance to express reality's deepest meanings in both public and private ceremonies. The modern "powwow" is a festival centered around dancing that has spread since World War II from the Plains tribes to Native American communities from coast to coast.

The Earth is our Mother.
The Sun is our Father.

—Okanagan saying

with water in all directions, and she knew that others with great power lived in this Fourth World. To the east was Talking God, to the west was House God, to the south was First Bringer of Seeds, and to the north was Second Bringer of Seeds. Begochiddy greeted each of them, and they made the waters recede, leaving the world deep in mud.

Begochiddy went back down to talk to the other people and tell them about the Fourth World. "Grandparent," they asked him, "what is it like?"

"It is good," she answered, "but it is wet and muddy. Someone must try to walk up there. Who will try first?"

Badger offered to go—but when he tried to walk on the surface of the Fourth World, he broke through into the mud. To this day, badgers still have black feet from the thick mud of the Fourth World when it was new.

The Navajo people call themselves the *Dine*, a word that means simply "people." There are more Navajos than there are members of any other North American tribe. Made up of more than 200,000 people, most of their tribe lives in the states of New Mexico, Arizona, Colorado, and Utah, where the huge Navajo Reservation covers more than 15 million acres. The Navajo believe that balance and beauty are the same thing, and that balance is the natural human state.

"Who will help me dry the Fourth World?" Begochiddy asked.

"We will," the winds answered, and they swirled and whirled across the surface of the Fourth World until the mud was dry. First the Ant climbed up and walked around, and then Begochiddy followed him to put things in order.

Begochiddy put everything where it belonged. He put the mountains in their places, and he set the Sun and Moon and Stars where they belonged in the sky. She taught the human creatures how to live, how to give thanks, and how to care for their plants. Begochiddy also gave them many different languages, and scattered them across Fourth World.

That is how our world came to be. However, one day, when human beings knock things too far out of balance, this world too will be destroyed.

ALTHOUGH Native Americans are made up of many tribes, each with their own folklore, this Navajo creation story tells us a great deal about the first North Americans. These long-ago immigrants came to North America thousands of years ago, crossing from Asia over the Bering Strait, and then gradually spreading across the continent. (The Navajo people traveled from Alaska to the Southwest about 700 or

For centuries, American Indians have believed that eagles and other animals possess powerful spirits.

800 years ago, just a few centuries before the European migration.)

This voyage from "world" to "world" may have influenced their creation stories about a series of worlds. Their ancient Asian roots also continued to influence them as they settled into the new land. They brought with them many of the legends and beliefs from Central Asia—but the new environment found in North America transformed this folklore, and the animals and landscape of their new home became part of their stories and traditions. In North America, the *animism* of Central Asia began to be expressed through stories about a land inhabited by spirits of great power. In the new stories Native Americans told each other, sometimes the land was it-

[Native Americans] developed ways of living and ways of teaching that enabled them to blend into the land, to sustain not just themselves, but generations to come. It is commonly said among the native people of the Northeast, for example, that we must always consider the results of our deeds on the seventh generation after our own. The knowledge that native people obtained from thousands of years of living and seeking balance, was, in a very real sense, quite scientific. But it was not taught to their people in classrooms or in books; instead, it was taught in two very powerful ways. The first way was through experience, the second through oral tradition, especially through the telling of stories.

—Joseph Bruchac, *Native American Stories*

The "potlatch" is a native ceremony that was common among the people who live along the west coast of North America from Oregon north to Alaska. The celebration was both a big feast and a gift-giving ritual; in fact, the word *potlatch* was given to the ceremony by white observers who heard the word *pa-chitte* ("to give") so many times that they thought this was the name of the ceremony.

The potlatch was of primary importance in the native economic, social, and political system. It provided an opportunity for people to trade goods and exchange stories. Weddings and births were celebrated during potlatches, and people feasted, danced, and were knit together in celebration.

self the bodies of these spirits. Everything was alive; everything was connected.

The Hopi god Kokopelli is an example of one of these spirits. According to legend, when the Hopi people entered this, the fourth world, they were met by an eagle who shot an arrow into the insect that carried the power of heat. The insect immediately began playing such powerful melodies on his flute that he healed his own pierced body. He then began scattering seeds of fruits and vegetables on the barren land, play-  ing his flute to bring warmth and make the seeds grow. The name Kokopelli was given to him, referring to the "hump" of seeds he carried on his back, and he be- came a symbol of happiness and joy. His flute could be heard in the spring breeze, bringing warmth after the winter cold.

Today, there are many native tribes across North America—but one thing they all share is a sense of their relationship to the Earth. They see their connection to the

rest of creation in terms of family. As a result, they look on the Earth in a very different way from most Europeans. For Native Americans, the Earth is the Mother of human beings. They honor her and love her and care for her, just as they would a human mother; they do not use her or buy and sell her. Many Europeans interpreted their religious stories to mean that they were the Earth's rulers, but American Indians saw themselves as Keepers of the Earth, entrusted with keeping creation in balance. Their ancient traditions are built on this view of themselves.

In today's world, the belief systems and traditions of many Native American groups have been eroded by modern society. Tribes across North America, however, are struggling to hold on to their identities by keeping the old customs alive.

Storytelling is one of the most important of these customs. The storyteller has an important and irreplaceable function in American Indian life, for he or she gives life to an ancient worldview. According to Native American folk traditions, storytellers are both artists and magicians; they keep the realms of the past and the sacred alive. They teach and they inspire; they affirm identity and meaning.

The Iroquois of the Northeast believed that *orenda* flowed through all things, a life force or power that connected plants, earth, animals, and humans. The Algonquian Indians had a similar concept, called *manitou*, a word that means both "wonderful" and "life." Because of this belief, in native traditions inanimate things are charged with life. A stick may become an **amulet**, for instance, and a place a sacred site.

The ancient Celts' designs reflect their belief in the interconnectedness of all life.

THREE

Celtic Folklore
The Ancient Heritage of the British Isles

The folktale of strange green children tells us about the Celtic worldview.

Long, long ago in the 12th century, in the midst of a civil war between England's King Stephen and the Empress Matilda, two strange green children wandered from their own land into the county of Suffolk. They were first seen crawling out of a hole in the ground where a tree had been uprooted on the land of Sir Richard de Calne, a Norman knight. The peasant folk who lived in the area were frightened and fascinated by the children's pale green skin. They captured the children and brought them to Sir Richard.

Sir Richard asked everyone he knew about the children, hoping that someone would know their story. He could not ask the children themselves, because they spoke a peculiar language no one could understand. Obviously confused and frightened by their surroundings, they refused to eat anything but vegetables and other plant foods, and they grew thin and weak.

Sir Richard adopted the children as his own **wards**, and he placed them under the care of the priest in his household. The boy continued to waste away, and he soon died, but the girl thrived. With Sir Richard and the priest's help, she learned English and was able to tell her story.

She and her brother came from the Otherworld where everything was green: the sky, the earth, the people, the animals. Just as in England, the people there lived in small farming communities, but no day and night existed, for the sun never shone. The air was constantly misty and wet, and plants grew luxuriously. No one ate meat there but only grass and other plants. They worshipped the gods in the old way, the way England had known before the coming of Christianity.

The girl told Sir Richard that she and her brother had wandered into the upper world by mistake—and a flood in their own world had washed away the hole between the worlds, trapping them here. Sir Richard's priest wrote down everything the girl said, but he buried the account, for fear that the story was "unchristian."

The girl grew up happily enough. She enjoyed learning and she grew to love the Christian faith, since it fit easily with the beliefs she had been taught in her own land. When she became a young woman, she married one of Sir Richard's squires and moved away from the area.

But something about Sir Richard's lands drew her back again and again . . . and one day she simply disappeared. The peasant folk knew she had gone back to her old world, leaving only her memory behind. They told her story to each other over and over—and hundreds of years later, their descendents brought the story with them when they immigrated to the New World.

TODAY Celtic folklore and traditions continue to play a part in the culture of people from the British Isles, especially those from Ireland, Scotland, and Wales. As this folk story indicates, a belief in a supernatural world, a world with passageways to our own, was an important element of the Celtic tradition. According to this way of thinking, our world was full of "thin places," spots where the supernatural world was so close that be-

ings from either side could easily break through into the other realm.

Originally, the Celts were an ancient people who traveled west into Europe to settle throughout the continent. The Roman Empire pushed them ever westward, until at last only pockets of them were left in the British Isles and in Brittany. They were never a unified nation, and even their name—*keltoi*—meant simply "secret" or "hidden." Their traditions, however, have never quite been completely erased from the earth.

When Christianity came to their lands, many of the Celts, like the strange green girl in the story, welcomed the new faith. Christian concepts made sense to them: they were already familiar with Heaven's otherworld; they already believed in Christianity's immortality; they inhabited a friendly, **animate** world that easily accommo-

The Irish called the fairy world Tír na nÓg. It was said to have been created by the greatest of all Irish folk saints, Saint Patrick, who banished the fairy people to an underground world where time flowed differently from the upper world.

The Welsh called the otherworld the Kingdom of Annwn. This was originally seen as a place of contentment, learning, and rest, a "place of the Blest," but as **fundamentalist** Christianity spread through Wales in the 18th and 19th centuries, the mythical realm began to be equated with Hell.

dated the supernatural presence of Christ and the saints; and Christianity's three-person God made perfect sense to a people who believed that the number three was sacred. Where Roman Christianity had tried to erase the old pagan beliefs, Celtic Christianity embraced the old beliefs with the new, enriching each with the traditions and symbols of the other.

The influence of Celtic folklore can be seen in many of today popular fantasy books—for instance, J.R.R. Tolkien's *The Lord of the Rings* and J. K. Rowling's Harry Potter books.

Like Native American traditions, Celtic folklore carried this message: the earth and human beings are linked together in a loving relationship. For the Celts, the earth is blessed and holy, charged with a living and holy presence. One of the most ancient Celtic Christian poems, "The Cry of the Deer," traditionally attributed to Saint Patrick, describes the earth's relation to the individual in these terms:

I arise today
Through the strength of heaven;
Light of sun,
Radiance of moon,
Splendour of fire;
Speed of lightning,
Swiftness of wind,
Depth of sea,
Stability of earth,
Firmness of rock. . .

According to Celtic folk traditions, reality cannot be divided into two pieces, the secular and the religious. Instead, all of reality is one piece, all blessed.

The echoes of these traditions are often faint today. North American immigrants from the British Isles carried with them many Celtic stories and ideas, but these were mixed with the traditions of the other cultures who had settled Britain along with the Celts. The Celtic voice grew fainter still as it was overpowered by the voice of the Roman Catholic Church.

And yet Celtic folklore is accommodating, and in many cases, it simply mixed itself in with the other ingredients, as folklore so often does. One Irish author, F. Delaney, describes his background this way:

In my Irish Catholic boyhood we drank a curious soup of religion and mythology, rich and . . . comforting yet warming. The ingredients . . . were the sober Christianity of Patrick and the wild paganism of the Celts. So close the relationship, so alive the pagan history . . . , that if a bunch of time-travelling, horse-borne Celtic warriors had turned up at Mass on a Sunday morning my eyes would have been surprised—but not my imagination, nor my faith.

In the New World, Celtic folklore lived on most strongly in isolated pockets—like Newfoundland in Canada and Appalachia in the

Tales of King Arthur and his knights are often based in Celtic folktales.

Apparently, the New World has its own openings into the Otherworld. Students in Newfoundland, Canada, collected 20th-century accounts of people who said they had encountered fairies or other supernatural folk. These encounters often took place in the deep woods of Newfoundland, far from human habitation. People who met the fairyfolk were often said to be forever "changed" in some mysterious way.

United States, places where tight-knit communities of settlers lived for centuries with little contact with the outside world. There, supernatural creatures (like fairies and elves) and doors that cracked open between the worlds continued to be realities, traditions that had been handed down from generation to generation.

The Celtic traditions may seem faraway from North American culture as a whole—and yet we catch a glimpse of them on St. Patrick's Day, when we see pictures of leprechauns, the little green magical folk that seem to have somehow made it across the Atlantic Ocean. Many of the fairytales that continue to inspire fiction and films have their roots in Celtic folklore.

The story of King Arthur, for instance, is deeply rooted in Celtic folklore (although the historical Arthur may have been Roman), and this story grasps North Americans' imaginations, inspiring filmmakers and novelists to create ever-new versions of the ancient tale. Arthur's wise and mysterious power points toward an ideal kingdom, one that North Americans cannot seem to completely forget.

This world of secrets and possibility, of wonder and blessing continues to enchant North Americans. It offers us an alternative to the everyday world of machines and finances, rush-hour traffic and work responsibilities. In this alternative world there is no need to outgrow the fascination we feel for quests and heroes, elves and magicians. We may be able to barely hear the echo from Celtic folklore's long-ago voice, but it is still there, sweet and faraway, telling us of that magic just might be real after all.

> There was no limit to the . . . Otherworld. It was, in effect, the land of Celtic imagination and the land of longing and desire. Each time we pick up a fairy-story like "Jack in the Beanstalk," or read a tale of fantasy, we enter that strange country that was so real to our ancestors.
>
> —Bob Curran, *Celtic Mythology*

The images of Africa came with the slaves to the New World.

FOUR

African American Folklore
The Power to Fly

Stories of miraculous flight gave early African Americans hope.

SHORTLY BEFORE the Civil War, a boatload of seven or eight slaves were shipped down from Savannah to a smaller town in Georgia. These slaves had been born in Africa, and they didn't speak English; instead, they spoke a language that sounded like ducks quacking to those who had been born in the New World.

Mr. Blue was the overseer where these slaves were sent; he ordered them out to the field, but he couldn't make them work. No matter how hard he tried, they couldn't understand what he wanted them to do.

So one morning, Mr. Blue headed out to the field with a whip in his hand. He cracked it as hard as he could over the heads of the new slaves; he caught them across the back next and then across their faces and sent lines of red blood springing up against their skin. The new slaves huddled together in a circle. One of them stuck a hoe in the ground—and then, to the amazement of everyone there, the whole bunch of them rose up in the air and flew like birds, over Mr. Blue's head, away toward Africa. No one ever saw them again.

BACK in the 1940s, an old man named Wallace Quarterman told this story to the Georgia Writers' Project. He had been at town when the amazing event happened, he said, but he knew plenty of people who had witnessed those slaves flying away through the sky, leaving the hoe standing in the ground beneath them.

Mr. Quarterman wasn't the only one to tell a similar story. Other old people in Georgia recalled hearing of slaves fresh from

Africa who simply flew away when the master tried to make them work. One group, said Priscilla McCullough, formed a circle and spun faster and faster, until one by one each rose into the air and took wing like a bird. The overseer grabbed the last one by the foot; Priscilla didn't know if he was able to pull the person back to the ground, but she knew the others got away and were never seen again.

During the **Depression** era, the Works Progress Administration sponsored the Federal Writers' Project, a program that sent writers' into the South (among other places) to collect oral narratives from ex-slaves.

Flight was a persistent image in African American folklore. For a group of people who were initially enslaved and then continued to be oppressed within North American society, flight was an image of hope and inspiration. It said to African Americans that it was possible to rise above the white oppressors; it gave African Americans a stubborn and invincible faith that endured despite the hardship of their existence.

In these folk stories, individuals actually flew back to Africa, but for those who were left behind, the traditions of Africa gave them a different sort of wings: the inspiration to hold on to their identities and keep their integrity. Even today, African American folklore continues to be deeply rooted in African stories and traditions.

Like the folklore of Native Americans, African folktales are full of animal characters that combine power with trickery. The Africans brought with them to the New World stories of Anansi, the spider-trickster (sometimes called Aunt Nancy in the slave dialects of the South). In North American folklore, Anansi the spider blended with another trickster character—Br'er Rabbit. Both were small and apparently powerless animals, but both Anansi and Br'er

Rabbit, in story after story, managed to outwit those who seemed to be more powerful. Just as stories of flight gave African Americans hope and dignity, so did these stories of clever and invincible tricksters.

Br'er Rabbit had many adventures with his other animal friends—and he didn't *always* win, especially when he matched wits with Br'er Wolf. For instance, one day Br'er Rabbit saw that Br'er Wolf had a magic hoe that dug the earth all by itself whenever Br'er Wolf said "Swish"—and Br'er Rabbit determined that

---

Food is an important aspect of folklore, one that gives an ethnic group comfort and a sense of belonging. Yams are a common African American food, used in a variety of ways, including sweet potato pudding.

To make the pudding:

Boil 6 yams until soft. Cool, peel, and cut into small pieces. Combine with:

¾ cup of sugar
2 eggs
2 tsps vanilla
½ tsp nutmeg
½ tsp cinnamon
½ tsp baking powder
½ stick of butter
1 cup of evaporated milk

Beat until smooth. Bake in a 350-degree oven for 45 minutes.

Other African American folktales tell of slaves returning to Africa by other means than flying. According to some accounts, a group of slaves arrived at a plantation weighted down with chains and iron around their necks, wrists, and ankles. Miraculously, despite their bonds, they simply turned away from their captors and walked down the river—on the water! The white folk were left with their mouths hanging open, listening to the faint sounds of joyful singing as it floated back to them over the water.

he had to have the hoe for himself. So one day when Br'er Wolf was away, Br'er Rabbit stole the hoe and took it to his field.

"Swish!" he said, and the hoe began to dig. It worked and worked and dug up all the weeds. But it didn't stop then. Instead, it just kept on digging and digging and digging, until all the crop was gone too. Br'er Rabbit kept yelling, "Swish, swish!" but the more he yelled the more the hoe worked.

Finally, Br'er Wolf came along. Br'er Rabbit begged him to help, but Br'er Wolf was mad at Br'er Rabbit for stealing the hoe. After a good long time, he took pity on Br'er Rabbit and said, "Slow, boy." The hoe dropped to the ground, and Br'er Wolf carried it back to his own field.

Some of the people inter-

> Stripped of family and friends, every possible belonging, even language, name, and religion, the kidnapped Africans did manage to smuggle a few revered comrades aboard the slave ships that transported them to America: Br'er Rabbir and Br'er Anancy. . . [who] became their models for the indirection, trickery, masking, and verbal dexterity that the enslaved men and women would have to bring into play to survive with some sense of dignity.
>
> —Daryl Cumber Dance, *From My People*

viewed in the '40s by the Georgia Writers' Project told about a magic hoe like Br'er Wolf's, one they had heard could work the earth all by itself if you knew the magic word. The hoe was clearly an important item in the African American imagination, a symbol for hard, unwanted labor. Their folk traditions once more gave them a way to rise above the everyday reality of their lives to a higher and more hopeful reality.

White North Americans did not encourage the African Americans' unique identity; they did what they could to erase it all together. Folklore is stubborn and deeply rooted, however. Although it is easily influenced and shaped, it resists efforts to change it artificially. African Americans' folklore allowed them to

> Br'er Rabbit's experience with the magic hoe is a lot like that of the magician's apprentice with his master's magic broom, a story that was used by Walt Disney in his movie *Fantasia*.

When early African Americans encountered Christianity, many biblical themes worked to give them a sense of their own value. They particularly identified with Old Testament stories of the Israelites' escape from slavery. Combining the rhythms and patterns of their homeland with stories they learned from the Bible, America's slaves created powerful songs of sorrow and hope.

Oh, Joshu-ay,
He prayed to God
To stop the sun
Right on the line.
An' the battle was foughten
Ten seven times.

An' the sun stop steady,
Sun stop steady,
Sun stop steady in the mornin'.

Oh, swing low, chariot,
Swing low, chariot,
Oh, swing low, chariot, in the morning.

I want to go to heaven,
Want to go to heaven,
Want to go to heaven in that mornin'.

Joshu-ay
Was the son of Nun,
And God was with him
Until his work was done.
God opened the window
And began to look out,
The ram horn blowed
And the children did shout,
The children did shout
Till the hour of seven,
Till the walls fell down
An' God heard it in Heaven.

Ah, weep on, Mary,
Weep on, Mary,
Oh, weep on, Mary in the mornin'.

African American folklore has been the inspiration for both literature and music. Novelist Zora Neale Hurston collected African American folklore, and poet Langston Hughes was inspired by African American folklore in much of his work. Contemporary authors like Toni Morrison and Alice Walker continue to use African American folklore to provide them with images and story ideas.

hold on to their roots, their identity, and their hope for the future.

In today's world, these ancient stories and traditions continue to offer strength and dignity. African American folklore tells us all that although our lives may be hard, we have the power to fly.

According to Norse legend, a great tree stands at the center of the universe. A serpent-dragon gnaws on the roots.

FIVE

The Folklore of Northern and Eastern Europe

The Struggle Between Life and Death

Scandinavian immigrants to North America continued to celebrate St. Lucy's Day, a mixture of Christian and ancient Norse folklore.

JUST AS THE EARTH rotates on its axis, long-ago Germanic and Scandinavian Europeans believed that our reality turns round an enormous tree. They called this tree Yggdrasil, a vast ash tree that fills not only the known world with its branches but is rooted in the deepest of the underworlds. It is the backbone of the universe, the structure that gives support to all of reality.

One of the tree's roots dug deep down into Jotunheim, the land of the Frost Giants. The second descended into Niflheim, where a snake-like dragon named Nidhogg feasted on the dead. Between bites, Nidhogg liked to gnaw on Yggdrasil's root; just for spite, he was trying to loosen up the world's firm and eternal structure. The third root burrowed into Asgard, the land of the gods. These roots symbolized the constant struggle between death and everlasting life, a struggle that lies at the heart of this world's reality.

Odin, the greatest of the gods, longed to understand the secret of this struggle. He craved wisdom so much that he hung himself from Yggdrasil for nine days. According to legend, he said of this experience, "I hung from that windswept tree, hung there for nine long nights. I was pierced by a spear. I was an offering to Odin, myself to myself. . . . Then I began to thrive, my wisdom grew. I prospered and was fruitful. One word gained me many words. One deed gained me many deeds."

In the end, Odin died on the cosmic tree—and then rose again, embodying in his own flesh the balance between life and death. The obvious parallels between his story and Christ's may have given Christianity an advantage when it spread to this part of the world.

In any event, by the time immigrants from Scandinavia, Germany, Poland, and other northeastern European nations settled in the New World, Christianity had almost erased the old Norse legends that once shaped such a large part of their folk-lore. But ethnic folklore is a little like the strong roots of Yggdrasil, buried deep in other worlds, and a people's ancient legends continue to influence the growth of younger folklore branches. The immigrants to North America brought with them customs and stories that grew from both the ancient Germanic legends and from the lore of the Church. St. Lucy celebrations are an example of such **hybrid** folk traditions.

According to Church folklore, Lucia came from a wealthy Sicilian family. In the days of early Christian persecution, she was said to carry food to Christians hiding in dark underground tunnels. To light the way, she wore a wreath of candles on her head. When she spurned a suitor's offer of marriage, he reported her to the local Roman authorities, who sentenced her to be removed to a brothel and forced into prostitution. According to legend, Lucia became immovable and could not be carried away. She was next condemned to death by fire, but she proved impervious to the flames. Somewhere along the way, her eyes were removed, and she is often portrayed carrying them in a platter. Finally, her neck was pierced by a sword and she died.

SAINT LUCY'S SONG

A Swedish community in Raleigh, North Carolina, celebrates
St. Lucy's Day by gathering around a young girl with lights in
her hair while singing this song in Swedish:

The night goes with weighty step
'round yard and stove;
'round earth, the sun departs,
leaves the woods brooding.
There in our dark house,
appears with lighted candles
Saint Lucia, Saint Lucia.

The night goes great and mute.
Now one hears its wings
in every silent room
murmurs as if from wings.
Look at our threshold stands
white-clad with lights in her hair
Saint Lucia, Saint Lucia.

The darkness shall soon depart
from the earth's valleys;
thus she speaks
a wonderful word to us
The day shall rise anew
from the rosy sky.
Saint Lucia, Saint Lucia.

The ancient Norse—often called Vikings— wrote with runes. This rock carving tells the story of Odin.

On December 13th, many Scandinavian immigrants celebrated by having a young woman—the "Lucy bride"—go from one farm to the next at the break of dawn, dressed in a white gown with a red sash, wearing a crown of twigs and blazing candles, bringing baked goods to each home. In later years, the community tradition changed to a family custom, and on St. Lucy's Day the family daughter would bring "Lucy cats" (saffron buns) and coffee to wake the family.

The historical Lucia grew up far from northern and eastern Europe. She is one of the earliest Catholic saints, who was **martyred** in Italy in the sixth century after Christ. According to some **folklorists**, peaceful Viking traders to Italy brought the story of Saint Lucy back to their

St. Lucia bread may be shaped in many ways, including a crown, a cross, simple "S" figures (representing the eyes of St. Lucy), or a wreath. The lighted crown and saffron-colored dough are also said to symbolize that the sun will soon return. The buns called *Lusse-katter* ("Lucy-cats") look like wagons with four wheels.

> According to tradition, miracles occurred at midnight on St. Lucy's Eve. Those awake at this mysterious and powerful hour might hear cattle speaking or see running water turn into wine.

homelands. Church legend tells that when Sweden was in the grip of a terrible famine in the midst of a bitter winter, a ship sailed across Lake Vannern with a beautiful young woman dressed all in white at the helm. Saint Lucy had miraculously brought a shipload of wheat, saving the people from certain starvation.

Other folklorists, however, believe that St. Lucy's Day traditions are really a Christianized version of ancient Norse winter celebrations. Saint Lucy herself may have originally been one of the Norns, the Germanic goddesses of destiny, similar to the Fates of Greek mythology. These three sisters dwelled under one of Yggdrasil's great roots, and they ruled the destinies of the gods, the giants, the dwarfs, and humanity. Like Lucy, they were often depicted with a ship and horn full of wheat and fruit. In some northern European countries, they were thought to appear at the birth of a baby, "Light Mothers" who brought candles to illuminate the child's future. Still other folklorists connect Lucy to the Germanic goddess Freya (sometimes thought to be Odin's wife), who traveled across the sky in a carriage pulled by her cats.

Early Scandinavian immigrants to North American also practiced another custom on St. Lucy's Day: their children wrote the word *Lussi* ("Lucy" or "light") on doors, fences, and walls. In pre-Christian times, this practice may have announced to the spirits of winter that their reign was broken; the sun would return, the days would grow longer, and

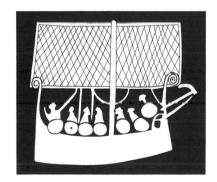

For the long-ago people of northern and eastern Europe, the Frost Giants represented the terrors of the natural world. Like Native Americans and the ancient Celts, these people believed that nature breathed with living spirits. The world where the Norse lived, however, was often hostile to human life. Steep, rocky mountains, icy storms, and avalanches of thundering snow were common realities in their world, and they believed that the spirits who inhabited Nature were mighty and menacing. In order to survive in such a mysterious and threatening world, human beings needed to be fierce and fearless.

humankind would survive yet another season of the Frost Giants' wrath.

For the people from northern and eastern Europe, North America offered hope and plenty. The land was wide and rich, the winter days were longer than the ones they knew in their homelands, and farms flourished. Many of these people settled in the north-central regions of what is now the United States, where the long, cold winters reminded them of their homelands. As they faced the challenges of their new home, their ethnic traditions gave them strength and an enduring sense of identity.

Although the Church's lore has tempered the fierce Germanic legends, this folklore is still

An old Scandinavian custom forbade all turning motions on St. Lucy's Day, including spinning, stirring, and working a grindstone. Superstitions warned that these circular motions might interfere with the sun's return.

one of vitality and courage. Like so much folklore, it tells us that in the struggle between life and death, darkness and light, ultimately life and light will triumph.

The Virgin of Guadalupe is a powerful religious figure that mixes European and Mexican folklore.

SIX

Hispanic Folklore
A Voice of Anguish

La Llorona is a symbol for Mexican Americans' identity.

ONCE LONG AGO in the Southwest, a beautiful woman and her three children were abandoned by her selfish lover. Left all alone, with no means to support herself and her children, the woman's sorrow and rage drove her insane. Seeking revenge against her children's father, in a moment of madness she threw them into the river and drowned them.

As soon as her sanity returned, she was overcome with guilt and anguish. The burden of what she had done was too great for her, and now her mind forever broke. Condemned to spend eternity searching for her dead children, her voice is often heard wailing through the night. Some have even caught glimpses of her floating above rivers or lakes as she searches endlessly for her little ones.

Throughout the Southwest, the legend of *La Llorona* ("the weeping woman") has endured for more than three centuries. Contemporary folklore still whispers of sightings. She has been seen trailing in her white dress through city streets and crying in the dark back roads of the country.

Sometimes La Llorona appears as a beautiful woman; other times, she may come to an unfaithful husband or lover as a horse-faced hag. Some Hispanic parents use her name to frighten their children into good behavior: "Behave yourself! La Llorona is coming." Almost every Mexican American has heard a form of her story; she lingers in the folk memories of generations.

This ancient tragic figure also symbolizes the blend of European and Native American cultures. When the Spanish first colonized the Southwest in the 1500s, they interbred with the native

La Malinche lived from 1502 to 1528. Her real name was Malintzin Tenépal, and although she was a princess, she was sold into slavery by her own mother. Since she spoke many of the native Mexican languages, Cortés used her as his translator. She gave birth to the first **mestizo**, and so she is considered to be the mother of *la raza cósmica* (the cosmic race). However, she is also seen as a double-crosser, for she warned Cortés of a planned ambush, saving his life and causing the massacre of thousands of her own people.

people, eventually creating a new ethnic group, one that was a mixture of two cultures. These early **conquistadors** and colonists may have brought the story of La Llorona with them—but they also found a version of the story already in the New World. According to Aztec legend, the goddess Cihuacoatl carries a dead baby cradled in her arms as she roams the countryside at night. A primary source recorded that before the coming of the Spaniards, the natives often heard at night "the voice of a woman who cried out in a loud voice, drowning herself with her tears, and with great sobs and sighs, wailing." In some versions of La Llorona's story, she was La Malinche, the native mistress of Cortés. When he abandoned her, she threw their son into the river.

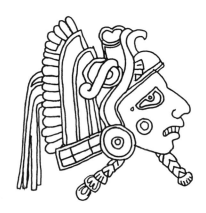

La Llorona is still a living part of

Symbols from ancient Mexico.

Huitzilopochtli, the Mexican god of war.

Leyendas (legends) are an important aspect of Hispanic folklore. These are oral narratives that are described as though they occurred in the recent past to a grandmother, cousin, parent, or friend; the narrator believes the story to be true. Because La Llorona's nighttime visits continue to be reported, she is considered to be a leyenda.

Mexican American folklore. Her story has inspired children's books, short stories, novels, and films; folklorists, anthropologists, and feminist writers continue to study this complex image. What's more, she also still makes regular appearances; Mexican Americans have reported seeing her in both urban and rural areas of the  Southwest, on college campuses, and even as far from her original home as cold windy Chicago.

La Llorona has become a cultural image, a metaphor for an entire people. Some Hispanic people see themselves as La Llorona's lost children, the offspring of the Spanish conquistadors and the native Indians. Although her story is tragic and eerie, ultimately she serves to give a sense of identity to a group of people who have often felt rejected by their deepest roots.

Her persistent tears have become the strong voice of the Mexican people, a people of dignity and history who have the courage to rise above their bitter beginnings.

The Torah is a vital part of Jewish life.

SEVEN

Jewish Folklore
Repairing a Broken World

For Jews, the act of binding phylacteries (leather boxes containing Scripture) to one's body symbolizes the importance of Scripture to everyday life.

For CENTURIES, despite being spread across the globe, the Jewish people have kept their culture alive. Their folklore has been handed down from generation to generation, preserving an ancient way of looking at the world and God. When many Jews immigrated to North America in the 19th century, they continued to stay true to their ancient identity. They fled the Old World looking for religious freedom and the chance to seek their fortunes in the new land of opportunity, and across North America, they thrived, despite the prejudice they sometimes encountered. Folktales like the one that follows were an important way to pass their culture on to new generations.

Once a rich man had three sons. Two left home to seek their fortunes; the oldest did well and gained riches of his own, but the second son lost everything and became a pauper. Many years passed—and then the rich man wrote to the oldest son, asking him to come home for the wedding of their youngest brother.

"Be sure to bring your brother home with you so we may all rejoice together," the letter said. "I promise to pay any expense you incur while fulfilling the commandment to honor your father and your mother."

The wealthy son immediately began getting ready for the wedding of his youngest brother. He dressed himself and his family in the most expensive clothes; then he sent for his poor brother.

The poor brother arrived at his door just as the rich brother

There is no folklore that can claim such a long and continuous history as the Jewish, that has had such a vast range of productivity and geography. It is richly varied and colorful with the imprint of the many diverse cultures that Jews have assimilated everywhere through the many centuries. Nonetheless, despite the absorption and adaptation on non-Jewish elements from without and despite the consequences of more than twenty-five centuries of wide dispersion in almost every part of the world, Jewish folklore probably possesses an over-all unity greater than that of any other.

—*Nathan Ausabel*

was ready to set out on the journey to their father's house. "What do you want?" the poor brother asked. "I haven't heard from you in all these years. Why the sudden interest in my presence?"

"Ask no questions," the rich brother snapped. "Come along now. We must be on our way."

"Where?" the poor brother asked. He looked down at his dirty rags, embarrassed to venture on a journey with his richly dressed brother. However, he had no choice; the rich brother gave him a shove, and they set off on their way.

When they arrived at their father's house, everyone turned out to welcome them. The wealthy son

and his well-dressed family walked proudly through the crowd. "Look at him," whispered everyone. "He looks like a prince."

Meanwhile, the poor brother slunk through the people, hoping no one would notice him. "Who is that?" whispered the crowd. "Surely he can't be from the same family?"

The brothers went on to the father's house, where they celebrated and partied for two weeks in honor of the younger son's wedding. At last, the oldest brother came to his father to say good-bye.

"Father, I have obeyed your letter, but now I must return home. As you know, I am an important man, and I have to attend to my business."

"Do what is best for you," his father answered.

The son waited expectantly, hoping that his father would now offer to pay his expenses as he had promised in his letter, but his father said nothing more. At last, the son handed his father an itemized bill, listing the cost of his clothes, his wife's clothes, his children's clothes, and all their travel expenses.

His father glanced at the list. "Wonderful!" he exclaimed. "I am happy for you, son, for I see you can afford to buy your family the finest luxuries. May you enjoy them in good health!"

"But, Father," the oldest son stammered, "you promised to reimburse me for all my expenses if I came to my brother's wedding."

The man stared at his son in surprise. "I never made such a promise."

"Yes, you did!" The son handed his father the letter. "See?"

The father took the letter and read out loud: " 'I promise to pay any expenses you incur while fulfilling the commandment to honor your father and mother.' "

"There!" the rich son cried. "You see?"

The father shook his head. "I promised to pay for whatever costs you encountered while honoring me and your mother. Had you really wanted to honor me, however, you would not have brought your poor brother here dressed in rags. Instead, you would have honored me by making sure that both my sons arrived dressed as would befit my family. Do you understand? All your expenses were for your own honor, not mine. And I promised you nothing for those expenses."

STORIES like these are an essential part of Jewish folklore. They teach each generation that the blessings of a Jewish heritage must be shared. Keeping the Sabbath and other traditional Jewish practices can be done in a way that honors only the individual—or it can be done in a way that honors God by doing good in the world.

Christian traditions often seek to **evangelize** the world, but the Jewish people have a different focus that centers on concrete action. They work in practical ways to repair a broken world—and stories are one of their most powerful tools.

The folklore of Southern European told of miracles in the midst of the ordinary lives of peasant farmers.

EIGHT

Southern European Folklore
In Search of a Better Life

Cemeteries are often the sites for supernatural events.

IN THE LATE 19TH and early 20th centuries, immigrants from Southern Europe flocked across the Atlantic to North America. They had heard that life was better in North America. As one woman told Elizabeth Mathias and Richard Raspa, authors of *Italian Folktales in America*, in North America "when you work you earned money and could eat and drink what you wanted. And there was freedom . . . no wars . . . no soldiers."

Many of the immigrants who arrived in American cities found that the Promised Land of plenty they had expected did not exist. Their new world had problems of its own—and many of the traditions of their old world were lost. They were used to life cycles that focused on planting and harvesting, weddings and funerals, baptisms and other religious celebrations. Now they had to accustom themselves to the patterns of a factory workday and the demands of their employers.

Ethnic neighborhoods within various cities gave these immigrants a sort of "shock absorber" against their new life, a way to live with others like themselves and hold onto some of their old traditions even as they adapted to the demands of their new homes. There they cooked the same foods, sang the same songs, and told the same stories as they had in their homelands. Some of them told the story that follows.

ONCE long ago there lived a kind priest who did everything he could to help the poor people in his community. He gave all his own belongings to the poor, and because he was filled with such love for others and such faith in the mercy and power of God, God granted him special powers. Through his prayers, he was able to order harmful things away to places where he willed them.

The priest made a habit of walking through the countryside, blessing fields and commanding storms to fall where they were most needed. One day, as he was walking through the fields, he passed a rich-looking stranger.

"A beautiful day, isn't it?" the priest murmured politely.

The stranger sneered. "It won't be for long."

"Oh, but it will be." The priest spoke with confidence, for he had just prayed that a heavy rainstorm be postponed until the young corn had grown strong enough to withstand the downpour.

"We'll see about that!"

The stranger looked so threatening that the priest decided to go home and devote himself to increased prayer.

But the priest found himself feeling very strange. He was so sleepy and weak that he knew he would have to go bed. Before he climbed into his bed, he called downstairs and told his house-keeper to wake him if she saw even the smallest cloud in the sky.

Religious faith and folk traditions are well mixed in Southern European cultures. Ethnic groups from this region often promise God they will build an altar to a favorite saint, if in return God will grant a particular favor. These homemade altars may be located in the yard—or an entire community may dedicate an altar to a parish's patron saint. A community altar like this serves as an ethnic iden-tity marker. Altars often contain religious figures and icons, as well as particular foods that have religious symbolism.

But his housekeeper felt sorry for him and let him sleep, even though dark clouds were piling up and moving closer. By the time the priest awakened, lightning was snapping across the sky. He jumped to his feet and tumbled down the stairs, scolding his housekeeper for not waking him. "Now it is too late!"

The priest stood outside staring up at the enormous cloud, praying for all he was worth. He commanded the cloud to rain only on the church cemetery, where it would harm no crops, but his power was not great enough to move the cloud. At last, he cried, "Oh God, my power is not enough. But I have faith that Yours is. Only You can save us now. Help me!"

With that, the cloud began to shrink until it was exactly the size of the church cemetery—and then enormous hailstones the size of hens' eggs tumbled out of the cloud onto the graves, rolling in great piles between the stones. The people ran to the priest and thanked him with tears of joy, but the priest could not stop staring at the mound of hailstones. "Dig down through the ice," he commanded his people, "and you will find the cause of this great storm."

Puzzled, the people obeyed their priest—and sure enough, beneath the ice, they found the figure of a well-dressed stranger.

Ever since the days of the medieval saints, the people of Southern Europe have told stories of miraculous happenings having to do with the dead bodies of holy people. Some bodies, like the good priest's, disappeared, indicating that the person had been miraculously assumed into heaven. Other times, years after the person's death, when the body was dug up for one reason or another, the corpse would be found to have not decomposed at all. According to folk traditions, the dead bodies of these saintly people often gave off a sweet smell like flowers. Sometimes a miraculous shape or image would be found imprinted on the body's face, heart, or hands.

He was as black as the devil—and quite dead. They knew he must have been a witch, and they buried him outside the churchyard.

By now, the priest was so weak he could barely stand. His people helped him back to his bed, but he grew weaker and weaker, and finally he died, a peaceful smile on his face. They put him in a coffin and prayed over him—but when they carried the coffin to the cemetery, it was so light, they knew he had gone to heaven, both in soul and in body.

FOR people from southern Europe, both Italians and Greeks, religion was an important part of their ongoing traditions in the New World. Religion and folklore were woven together, both vital parts of their everyday lives, and both gave them the strength they needed for the challenges of their new lives.

In a world where people worked in factories rather than on farms, the stories people told began to gradually change. The

Food is an important aspect of both Greek and Italian folklore. Special foods are sources of ethnic pride that help to communicate identity to members of the community. In North America, however, these foods are also appreciated by other members of the population. Italian food in particular has become a popular North American fare.

story of the good priest was still retold, but it no longer had the immediacy it had had back in Europe, for few immigrants from Southern Europe depended on the weather and the fields for their livelihoods.

But elements of the story made their way into new stories. One person might recount the story of a dark stranger who would have cursed his cousin's community but for the prayers of the priest; another person might remember that when her brother's coffin was carried to the cemetery it was so light they knew he had gone straight to heaven, body and all.

Living in an often harsh, industrial world, folklore's ancient traditions not only gave strength to these communities of immigrants; it also offered them hope. Divine power and supernatural grace were the same in the New World as it was in the Old. God was still on their side.

Some Greek Americans believe in the "evil eye"—the power to inflict harm merely by looking. Wearing or eating garlic is thought to protect against the evil eye, but avoiding envy and undue admiration is the safest form of protection.

Many French immigrants to North America were hunters and trappers.

NINE

French American
Folklore
An Identity All Their Own

The lonely life in the forests encouraged the imaginations of some French immigrants to the New World.

ONCE UPON A TIME there were three brothers who heard that the king of the land would give his daughter in marriage to whoever could make a boat that would sail on land or sea. So the oldest of the brothers decided to go into the forest and try to make a boat that would sail on land or sea. He took with him some biscuits, in case he got hungry, and set off on his way.

When he reached the woods, he passed an old woman who called to him, "Oh, young man, where are you going?"

"None of your business," answered the first brother. But the old woman stood in his way, and so he lied, "I'm going to make some wooden plates, old witch."

"Well, then," cackled the old woman, "I wish you plenty of plates."

The first brother continued on his way—but when he began to cut down trees to build a boat, the wood instantly turned into piles of wooden plates. No matter how much he chopped, all he could make was plates, so at last he gave up and went home.

The next day, the second brother packed himself a lunch of biscuits and set off into the woods to try his hand at making a boat that could sail on land or sea. He too met the old woman, who cried, "Hello, young man! What are you doing?"

"I'm off to make my mother some wooden spoons," the boy lied. "Not that it's any of your concern, you old hag."

"Well," the old woman said sweetly, "I wish you many wooden spoons for your efforts."

The second brother continued on his way—but when he set to chopping down trees, he found that the wood turned right

Tales of a magical flying canoe are common in French Canada.

away into spoons. After several hours of chopping, all he had was a pile of wooden spoons, so he went back home.

The third brother made his way into the woods the next day, and like his brothers, he too met the old woman. "Good morning, young man," she called.

"Good morning, Grandmother," he answered politely.

The old woman smiled. "Would you have any food you might share with a hungry old woman?"

The youngest brother opened his pack and took out the biscuits he had packed for his lunch. "Here you go, Grandmother," he said. "Help yourself."

The old woman took a small piece, but the boy pressed her to take more. "No, no," she said. "I just wanted to see what you would do. Where are you off to?"

French Canadians were expelled by the British from Acadia, Nova Scotia, in 1755 and eventually settled in Louisiana, where earlier French immigrants had already settled. These "Acadians" came to be known as "Cajuns."

"I'm going to make a ship that can go on land and water," the youngest brother answered.

"Well," she smiled, "that is what I wish for you."

And so the youngest brother made a ship that sailed on land and water. The king gave the youngest brother the princess to marry—and of course they lived happily ever after.

THIS folktale came to the New World with the French immigrants who began settling North America in the 17th century. In many areas, the French communities were so absorbed into the rest of the population that they became nearly invisible, but in Quebec and other areas of eastern Canada, as well as in the state of Louisiana in the American South, the French culture retained a unique flavor all its own.

The story of the ship that could sail on land or sea was more than just fairytale. Many French settlers claimed to have actually seen the magical vessel sailing through the air. One early historian records the story of the *chasse-galerie* (the flying canoe), saying, "I have met more than one old voyageur who claimed to have seen the bark canoes travel in the air filled with the possessed, going to see their sweethearts, under the sponsorship of **Beelzebub**."

Crediting supernatural activity to the devil was one characteristic of French folk culture. The devil was prone to showing up in many settings, and parents used him to warn their children against wild behavior. In one story, the devil was said to have danced with a girl name Rose Latulippe, charming her with his suave dark beauty—until she caught a glimpse of his cloven hooves. Then he disappeared in a puff of foul smoke.

Music is an important way of keeping folklore alive, even though its meaning may be changed somewhat by new surroundings. Folklorist Edith Fowke notes: "The pioneer settlers . . . brought with them the thousands of songs then being sung in Europe, and made them part of their everyday life. . . . Many were a legacy from the *jongleurs* of medieval France and have remained unchanged since the sixteenth or seventeenth centuries. . . . The pioneer clearing his land with an axe sang of knights and princesses, and the [woodcutters] made the woods echo to the strains of a ballad about three damsels in beautiful old Rochelle."

The story of Rose Latulippe is told by French Canadians along the St. Lawrence River, as well as by Cajuns from Louisiana. Interestingly, the story of the devil at the dance is also a common folktale on the other side of North America in the Southwest, where Hispanic Americans tell another version of the same story.

The *loups-garous*—or werewolf—was a prominent feature in French folklore of North America. Werewolf stories were told—and are still being told—by people from Quebec to the bayous of Louisiana.

Versions of stories like these continue to be told by North Americans of French descent. Often the stories are told in little snippets, rather than as a long, cohesive tale, and the narrators speak as though the incidents had happened to a friend or family member. These oral traditions, as well as distinctive forms of music, food, and speech, help this group of people maintain a sense of heritage. They may no longer think of themselves as connected to the nation of France, but the unique folklore that has evolved in North America gives them an identity all their own.

Many Asian Americans first came to North America to help build the railroad lines.

TEN

Asian Folklore
Wisdom and Simple Goodness

The Chinese folktale of Wen Jeng reveals the philosophy of traditional Asian folklore.

Wen Jeng was well known for being an expert authority on the art of Feng Shui. This meant that he was able to understand all the subtle forces that come to play in a specific place, and he could perceive the best way to arrange things so that life would be good for the people who lived in that space. Although Wen Jeng was very wise, he was not particularly good tempered. He often resented the demands on his time that his knowledge brought him.

One day he was called to give advice about the best place for a grave, high up in the mountains. The journey to the gravesite and back was a long and difficult one, and by the time Wen Jeng came down from the mountain, he was exhausted. His eyes were caked with dust, and he was parched with thirst.

As he stumbled along, he passed a woman and her sons where they were winnowing grain. "Please," he gasped, "do you have any water you could give me?"

The woman immediately poured water from a pitcher into a small bowl. Then she picked up a handful of chaff and sprinkled it onto the water before she offered it to Wen Jeng.

Desperate with thirst, Wen Jeng took the bowl, but he was furious with the woman for putting chaff on his drink. He longed to gulp the water down, but instead he was forced to carefully blow the chaff away so that he could sip it, all the while wondering how he could take revenge on her. Once he had splashed the dust from his eyes, he noticed a small shabby shack in the distance. "Is that your home?" he asked.

She nodded. "It is falling down, but I cannot afford to repair

it. Three years ago, my husband died, and since then, life has been nothing but a struggle."

Wen Jeng gave a thin smile. "Your troubles are over. I am an expert on these matters, and I can see from here that the position of your home has brought you bad luck. Across the mountain, I saw today another house, an abandoned building where no one lives, where you would find much better fortune. You and your sons should move there."

The woman knelt in gratitude, and Wen Jeng went on his way, grunting his satisfaction to himself. He had found his revenge for the woman's insult, for he knew that at the house where he had sent the woman the Feng Shui was so bad that her sons would probably all die before they reached adulthood.

Several years later, while Wen Jeng was traveling to offer his advice at another site, he decided to check on the woman and see how his revenge was working out. To his surprise, he found that her new home was neat and clean, and the fields around it were fruitful and productive looking. The woman rushed out to meet him.

"Oh Great Master," she cried, "thanks to you our lives have changed. My sons are grown now, and two are entering the government

Wen Jeng was a wise but impatient man.

while the other is studying with a Master. The fields are so bountiful that I can afford to hire someone to work them now that my sons are gone. If you had not come along that day, who can say where I would be today?" She invited Wen Jeng to stay with her for the evening meal. Puzzled, Wen Jeng accepted her invitation, determined to find out what had happened.

After an excellent meal, he sat back and confessed, "I cannot understand why Heaven has blessed you so. I sent you to the worst place I had ever encountered in my entire career—and yet you have prospered."

The woman stared at him in dismay and confusion. "I thought I owed all my good fortune to you. Yet now you tell me you wished me ill. What did I do to make you so angry with me?"

Wen Jeng was somewhat embarrassed, but he still remembered the way she had slighted him by sprinkling chaff on his drink of water. When he reminded the woman of what she had done, however, she looked still more dismayed. "How could you think I would insult you? I knew you were desperate for water— and if you gulped the water down, it would not be good for you. So I sprinkled chaff on the water to slow you down. I knew it would be better for you if you had to drink in sips rather than gulps."

Wen Jeng's cross old face creased in a smile. "Despite my mean nature, Heaven saw fit to bless you. You are so full of goodness, that you attract good fortune. May you continue to be as blessed as you deserve to be."

Traditionally, Feng Shui is based on the belief that unseen energies called *ch'i* influence human lives. The practitioner of Feng Shui manipulates these energies to achieve the most beneficial effects.

IN the 19th century, the builders of the railroad across North America looked for strong workers to lay the rails. The Chinese proved to be some of the best workers for this enormous job, and immigrants from China began to flock to North America. Today people from  across Asia are important members of North American communities. They have enriched North American folklore with their food and traditions—and with stories like that of Wen Jeng.

Many Asians place great faith in Feng Shui, an ancient concept that is at least 5,000 years old. Today, many other North Americans are also interested in this practice, and it has gained a new place in the modern folklore of North America.

Some may consider Feng Shui to be superstition, a folk custom that has no relevance in our modern scientific world. However, psychologists who study architecture have noticed that certain structures, colors, and designs do have an effect on human emotions. More important, Feng Shui is

The story of Wen Jeng is a Taoist folktale. Taoists believe that long life and good fortune spring from a life of simplicity and nonassertive action. Like several other such folktales, the story mocks the very beliefs it endorses, reminding listeners that no single system of philosophy holds all the answers.

Harmony and balance are important to Asian life.

Historically, Asians have faced enormous prejudice in North America—and yet today, many North Americans have come to appreciate the Asian cultures that are part of their communities. As evidence of this new respect and appreciation, many North Americans are fascinated with aspects of Asian folklore, including food, fashion, dance, and various customs such as Feng Shui.

deeply rooted in the philosophical perspective that all things are interdependent, a perspective that is reinforced by modern physics, ecology, and other scientific studies.

The gentle irony of the folktale, however, reminds us all that simple goodness is more important than even the most complex wisdom.

Children absorb folklore from their parents—and then transform it a bit when they pass it on to the next generation.

ELEVEN

Parents and Children
Ethnic Roots Planted in
New Surroundings

Ethnic folklore in North America is like a child who takes with him something of both his parents.

A**S YOU CAN SEE**, the various North American ethnic populations—and there are many more than we can cover in this book—are not like little pieces of the Old Country, still existing though detached from the rest of the body. Instead, they are more like children.

For instance, when you were a child, you probably shared many things in common with your parents, including the language you spoke, the food you ate, the music you enjoyed, and the stories you knew. As you grow older, you still speak the same language as your parents—but your vocabulary may be slightly different from theirs, and you may have even learned a new language that your parents have never spoken. You may try new foods, different from the ones your mother serves at home, and although you still think there's nothing like your mother's cooking, you may come to enjoy these new foods as well. By the time you are an adolescent, your musical tastes may be very different from your parents', and while you still know the old stories they told you as a child, you also know new stories you've learned from your friends, from school, and from whatever new environments you've encountered.

The same sort of thing happens when immigrants settle in North America. Gradually, they stop being "immigrants," pieces of their parent countries, and they grow into something new, an ethnic culture embedded within North American culture as a whole, a separate identity that has formed new bonds with the world around it. This new identity is still tied in some ways to the parent country of course, just as you will always be con-

Your generation has its own folklore; your parents have shaped your stories, tastes, and behaviors, but you have created something new in your lives.

nected in some ways to your parents. The new ethnic culture has not lost the old traditions and memories that formed it, but it has been influenced by new ideas, new stories, and new surroundings.

Because of the new factors in your own life, you may choose to believe things about the world and God that are very different from what your parents believe—and yet in one way or another, your internal worldview will always be affected to some extent by your parents' beliefs. How you think about love and relationships, your concept of marriage and family, your perspective on death and the supernatural world, all of this is shaped by your original family's ideas. In a similar way, ethnic cultures may abandon the old religion and traditions practiced in their original homelands—and yet those religious beliefs will be transformed in some way and flavor their ongoing folklore.

You may think of folklore as being about superstition. If so, you may consider that it has little place in the modern world and little to offer. In reality, however, folklore is a vital part of the contemporary world—and it has much to offer.

For example, many ethnic groups in North America have faced prejudice and hardship at one time or another. The surrounding culture has not always welcomed them or appreciated

Nothing reinforces the kinship of humanity across oceans and time more than folklore.

—Daryl Cumber Dance, *From My People*

their differences. When that has occurred, folk traditions provide a source of comfort and strength, a way of holding on to what is most important despite the external pressure from an unfriendly society, a way to maintain dignity and identity in the face of destructive forces. Folklore acts as "glue," a force that pulls together and bonds the people who belong to a particular culture.

Folklore is also the vehicle for a culture's wisdom. It has to do with life's inner meaning; it helps us grasp what is most important to us; and it shows us how to live with each other in the best

Gypsies are an ethnic group that has remained distinct from the rest of the North American population. They do so by maintaining a set of strict traditions—and using a different set depending on whether they are dealing with members of their own community or members of the North American population as a whole.

TRADITIONAL GYPSY BEHAVIOR

Toward Insiders	Toward Outsiders
Hospitality	Unfriendliness
Cooperation	Exploitation
Lying prohibited	Lying permitted
Obey taboos and other folk customs	Conceal folk customs
Demonstrate modesty and chastity	Demonstrate exaggerated sex appeal and faked promiscuity

Adapted from Carol Silverman's "Strategies of Ethnic Adaptation: The Case of Gypsies in the United States" in *Creative Ethnicity,* Stephen Stern and John Allan Cicala, editors (Logan: Utah State University Press, 1991), p. 109.

Never forget that folklore is all around us. We have heard
its voice in the songs our mothers sang to us at bedtime
or the tales our fathers told while waiting for the fish to
bite. We can hear it in the voices of the old when their
memories return to them full of mystery and power.
Folklore lurks behind the names we choose for our
streets and baseball teams, hound dogs and race horses.
It is in the traditions that bring dried corn husks to every
door in November or encourage the child to write his
dreams to Santa Claus. Like a river that is fed from innu-
merable tiny streams and brooks, folklore takes its
strength from many sources and as it grows it carries all
of us, young and old alike, along its wayward journey.

—Kemp P. Battle, *Great American Folklore*

possible ways. In other words, folklore teaches us to be better
people—and it helps us to interact with a world that may not be
limited by our five senses.

Perhaps best of all, no matter the ethnic group to which we
each belong, we can learn from each other's folklore. Each culture has a new slant on the world, one that enriches and in-
structs the rest of us. By experiencing the stories, food, music,
or traditions of another culture, we have a chance to look at
the world with fresh eyes—and maybe see something we have
missed before.

When we experience the folklore of another culture we often discover something interesting as well: we are not so differ-

ent from one another as we thought. The more we look, the more we find parallels between two ethnic groups' stories and traditions. Perhaps this means we share common roots we never suspected.

Or maybe these parallels simply spring from the fact that we all have much in common. Differences can be celebrated and enjoyed through ethnic folklore—but ultimately we all belong to the human family.

Further Reading

Ancelet, Barry Jean. *Cajun and Creole Folktales*. New York: Garland, 1994.

Ausubel, Nathan. *A Treasury of Jewish Folklore*. New York: Crown, 2000.

Bierhorst, John. *Latin American Folktales*. New York: Pantheon, 2002.

Castro, Rafaela. *Chicano Folklore*. New York: Oxford, 2001.

Cotterell, Arthur. *Norse Mythology*. New York: Lorenz, 2001.

Courlander, Harold. *A Treasury of Afro-American Folklore*. New York: Marlowe, 1996.

Curran, Bob. *Celtic Mythology*. Chicago: Appletree, 2000.

Fowke, Edith. *Legends Told in Canada*. Toronto: Royal Canadian Museum, 1994.

Leeming, David and Jake Page. *Myths, Legends, and Folktales of America*. New York: Oxford, 1999.

Lin, Te. *Chinese Myths*. New York: McGraw-Hill, 2001.

Stewart, R. J. *Celtic Myths, Celtic Legends*. New York: Sterling, 1997.

For More Information

American Folklore Society
afsnet.org

Folk Life
www.crt.state.la.us/folklife

Folklore Society
www.folklore-society.com

FROG—Folk and Roots Online Guide
www.folkworld.de/frog/canfst.htm

Les Voyageurs
www.google.com

Glossary

Amulet An object possessing magical powers.

Animate Possessing life and spirit.

Animism The belief that the objects and forces of nature possess conscious life.

Beelzebub Another name for the devil.

Conquistadors The Spanish conquerors of the New World.

Evangelize To preach the gospel to others.

Fundamentalist Based on the basic teachings of the Bible (usually from a literal interpretation).

Homogeneous Uniformly the same throughout.

Hybrid The offspring of two different parents.

Martyred Put to death for a particular belief or faith.

Metaphor A word symbol that compares two different things in order to deepen our understanding.

Mestizo A person with mixed European and Native American ancestry.

Wards Persons (often children) under the protection of a guardian.

Index

Biographies

Ellyn Sanna has authored more than 50 books, including adult nonfiction, novels, young adult biographies, and gift books. She also works as a freelance editor and helps care for three children, a cat, a rabbit, a one-eyed hamster, two turtles, and a hermit crab.

Dr. Alan Jabbour is a folklorist who served as the founding director of the American Folklife Center at the Library of Congress from 1976 to 1999. Previously, he began the grant-giving program in folk arts at the National Endowment for the Arts (1974–76). A native of Jacksonville, Florida, he was trained at the University of Miami (B.A.) and Duke University (M.A., Ph.D.). A violinist from childhood on, he documented oldtime fiddling in the Upper South in the 1960s and 1970s. A specialist in instrumental folk music, he is known as a fiddler himself, an art he acquired directly from elderly fiddlers in North Carolina, Virginia, and West Virginia. He has taught folklore and folk music at UCLA and the University of Maryland and has published widely in the field.